This annual belongs to:

mason

EGMONT

We bring stories to life

First published in Great Britain 2015 by Egmont UK Limited,
The Yellow Building, 1 Nicholas Road, London W11 4AN

Written by Mara Alperin
Designed by Pritty Ramjee, Cassie Benjamin and Claire Yeo

HiT entertainment

ISBN 978 1 4052 7899 7
60315/1
Printed in Italy

Meet the Team

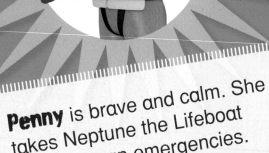

Fireman Sam is a hero! He is brave and strong. He drives Jupiter the Fire Engine!

Penny is brave and calm. She takes Neptune the Lifeboat out for ocean emergencies.

Elvis is a great firefighter who is always there to help. He likes to sing, too!

Station Officer Steele runs the Pontypandy Fire Station. **Radar** is a trained rescue dog who can sniff out trouble anywhere.

Tom Thomas runs the Mountain Rescue Centre. He drives the Rescue Jeep and pilots Wallaby One the Helicopter.

Coastguard Ben is the newest member of the team. He's a top sea rescuer!

Pontypandy Families and Friends

The Price family. Norman is always in trouble, so he's known as Naughty Norman! His mum, Dilys, owns the local store.

The Flood family. Mike is a handyman and Helen is a nurse. Mandy is Norman's best friend.

The Chen family. Mrs Chen is a teacher. Lily is very cute, but sometimes she gets in a lot of trouble!

The Sparkes family. Joe, Lizzie and Hannah are the newest family in Pontypandy. Joe runs the garage and loves to invent things. Hannah is a lot of fun!

The Jones family. Sarah and James are twins. They love adventures! Charlie has a fishing boat, and Bronwyn runs the Wholefish Café.

All About Titan

Titan is the new firefighting boat. Located at the Pontypandy Ocean Rescue Centre, Titan is always ready for a deep-sea rescue!

Titan's water cannons pump water straight from the ocean.

Always wear a life jacket when you're out at sea!

Ben is a fantastic coastguard. Circle the rescue equipment he needs, and cross out the things he doesn't need.

life ring

guitar

binoculars

life jacket

skateboard

Splash!

Titan can put out fires and rescue people who are lost at sea.

What colour is Titan?

All aboard! Who is ready for an ocean rescue? Point to each member of the team and say their names.

Ben

Elvis

Sam

Answers on page 67.

Story:
Escape from Pontypandy Island

Now read about Titan's exciting rescue!

The Pontypandy Pioneers were getting ready for a sailing trip with Trevor.

"I **can't wait** to explore Pontypandy Island," said Mandy.

James was running late. He was busy reading his new book, *How to be a Great Explorer*.

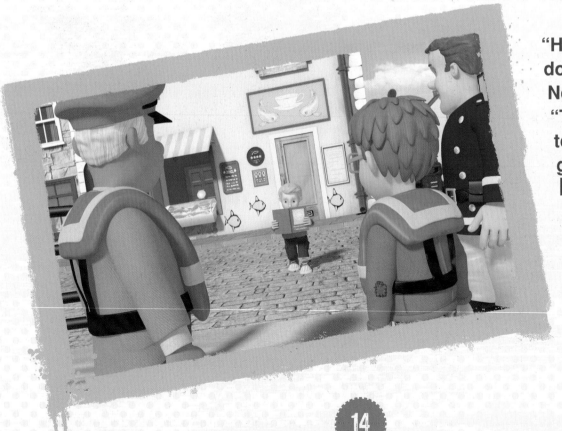

"Hah! Explorers don't need books," Norman laughed. "They just need to be brave. I'm going to be the **best explorer ever!**"

At Pontypandy Island, the Pioneers pulled the boat to shore. "Now can I go exploring?" Norman asked, impatiently.

"Wait a minute," said James. "My book says that the boat must be high on the shore. Or it might float away."

"I don't have time for books," said Norman. "I'm going to be the first to discover **something amazing**."

Norman, Mandy and Sarah ran off ... leaving the boat behind! It slowly drifted out into the water.

Before long, Norman spotted something out at sea. "Look!" he cried. "I see a boat! Small and white with a sail."

"Oh no!" gasped Trevor. "That's our boat. We're **stranded** on the island!"

James knew what to do. His book explained how to signal for help. He put grass and green sticks on the campfire. Then he waved the picnic blanket to make smoke signals.

Back at the Ocean Rescue Centre, Coastguard Ben saw the smoke. "The Pioneers must be in trouble," he said.

Penny jumped into **Neptune** and sped towards the island.

Meanwhile, Norman wanted to prove he was a good explorer, too. He threw more firewood onto the campfire to make an even bigger smoke signal.

"No, Norman!" shouted Trevor. But it was too late!

Suddenly, the bushes burst **into flames!**

"**Help**!" cried Norman. "What do we do?"

"My book says to move towards the water for safety," James read.

Penny arrived, and helped everyone safely into **Neptune**. "I'll call Fireman Sam to put out the fire," she said.

Back at the station, the alarm sounded. "Elvis, we're going to need **Titan**!" Sam said.

The Fire Crew raced towards Pontypandy Island.

"Let's move in!" Sam called.

Sam and Elvis used Titan's strong water cannons to put out the flames.

"Hooray!" everyone cheered.

On the way home, Penny rescued the sailboat.

"I'm sorry for causing the fire," Norman said. "I just wanted to be a **really good explorer!**"

"Great explorers know that safety always comes first," said Sam. "Well done, James. You were a true explorer today."

Sam presented James with a **special medal** for bravery.

"Thank you," James said. "But I couldn't have done it without my book!"

THE END

How to be a Great Explorer

You can be a great explorer, just like James! You can explore a park, your garden or even your house.

Just follow these tips:

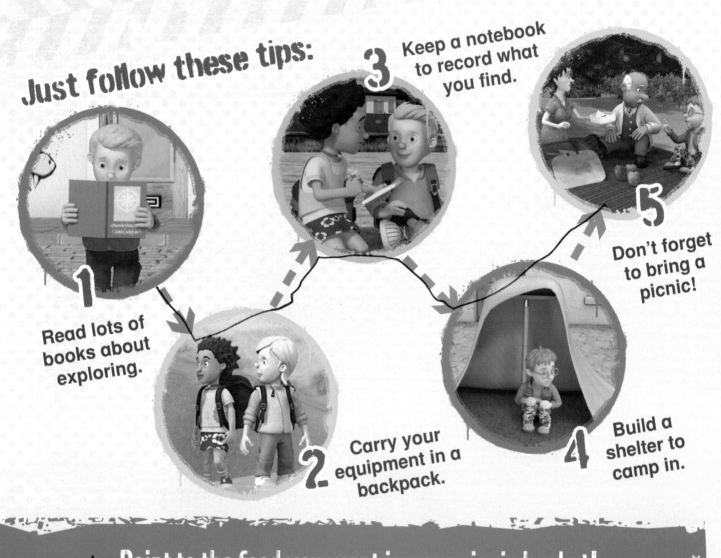

3 Keep a notebook to record what you find.

1 Read lots of books about exploring.

2 Carry your equipment in a backpack.

5 Don't forget to bring a picnic!

4 Build a shelter to camp in.

Point to the food you want in your picnic basket!

Action Stations, Go!

The rescue vehicles are ready for any emergency! Draw lines to match Venus, Neptune and Wallaby One to their shadows.

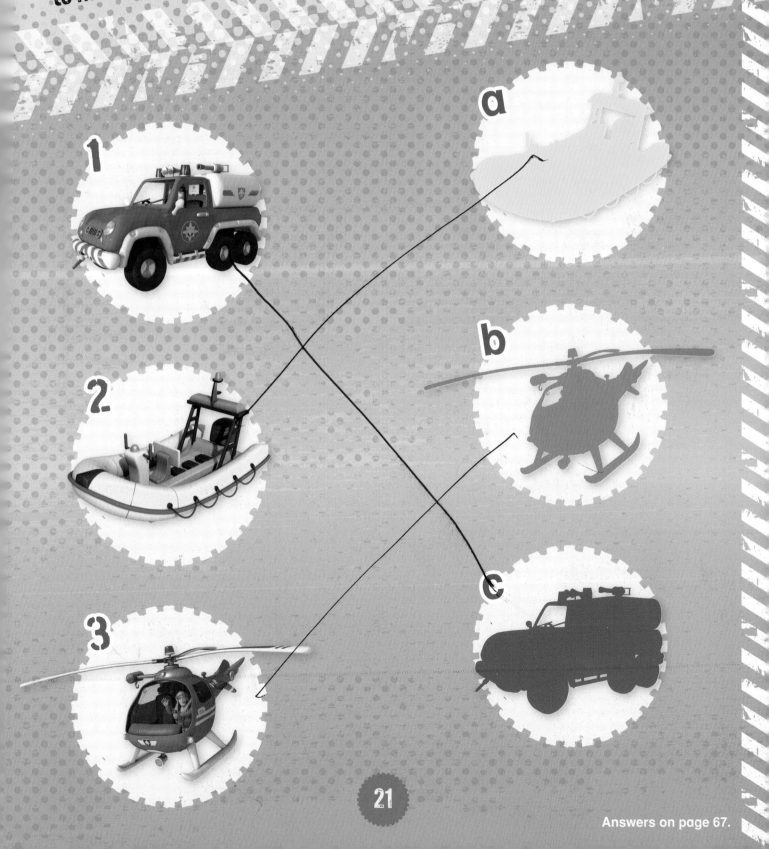

Answers on page 67.

Story:
Up, Up and Away!

Can you think of other things that can fly?

Read about Joe's hot-air balloon!

Joe likes to invent things. He's built a hot-air balloon! "It's amazing!" says Mandy. She loves hot-air balloons. "Can I fly in it?"

But before Mandy can go, Lambikins jumps in the basket. "Baa!" she bleats. She nibbles at the ropes, and the hot-air balloon takes off! "Come back, Lambikins!" cries Norman.

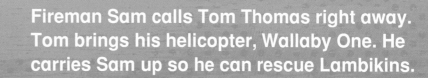

Fireman Sam calls Tom Thomas right away. Tom brings his helicopter, Wallaby One. He carries Sam up so he can rescue Lambikins.

Fireman Sam brings Lambikins safely back to the ground. Norman gives his pet a big cuddle. "No more flying for you!" he says.

THE END

Colouring Time

Use your brightest crayons to colour in this hot-air balloon!

If you could fly in a hot-air balloon, where would you go?

How should I decorate it?

What shape is the balloon?

Triangle

Circle

Square

24

Answers on page 67.

Radar to the Rescue

Charlie and James are lost in the fog.
Can Radar sniff them out?
Help guide Radar through the maze.

START

FINISH

Answers on page 67.

Spot the Difference

Say cheese! Can you spot five differences in Picture 2?

1

Colour in a star as you spot each change.

2

I just want a
cheese sandwich!

Write over the letters to discover what everyone is chasing after!

cheese

All About Jupiter

The Fire Crew drive Jupiter to rescues.

Jupiter's hoses spray water to put out fires.

Fireman Sam and Elvis put a fire out!

Colour in the splashes!

Jupiter's bright red paintwork is clean and shiny. It's a clear sign that help is on the way! Which other vehicle is red like Jupiter?

Rescue Jeep

Ambulance

Venus

28

Answers on page 67.

Nee Nah! Nee Nah!

Jupiter's flashing lights and sirens warn people to clear the way.

Can you make a noise like Jupiter?

1

2

3

4

5

How many sirens does Jupiter have? *Point to the right number.*

Action Stations, go!

Who is inside Jupiter? Point and say their names.

Elvis

Penny

Story: Record Breakers

One morning, Norman and Mandy were reading a story in the newspaper.

"Listen to this," said Mandy. "There's a boy in Newtown who balanced a ball on his nose for two hours. He's going to be in *The Gwyneth Book of Records*."

"I bet I could do it for **three** hours!" Norman bragged.

Mandy held the stopwatch while Norman wobbled back and forth.

"**Ohhhhhh,**" he cried, as the ball rolled off his nose.

"That's three and a half seconds," Mandy reported.

Norman sighed. Breaking the world record was going to be **much harder** than he had thought!

Then Norman had a new idea. "I'll find a better **world record** to break. *Gwyneth Book of Records* here I come!"

Norman tried stacking hats on his head. But he stumbled, and the hats **toppled** to the ground!

"How many was that?" he asked.

"Six hats, ha!" Mandy laughed. "A boy in Finland managed **thirty-eight**."

Just then, Norman's cousin Derek walked by. "What are you doing?" he asked Norman.

"I'm going to break a **world record**," Norman said proudly.

Derek smiled. "I bet I can break a world record before you can, Norman."

"Well I bet you can't," Norman replied.

Norman tied a bunch of balloons to a garden chair.

"Start the stopwatch, Mandy!" he said. "I'm doing a record breaking balloon flight!"

But before Norman could take off, a bird flew past and popped the balloons with her beak. *Pop! Pop!*

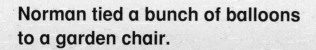

"My turn," said Derek. "Start the stopwatch – I'm going to break the pogo-ing record!"

Derek bounced three times ... and then he fell off. *Crash!*

"This is rubbish," said Derek, as he stormed off. "I'm going to break a more exciting world record!"

32

"Think, Mandy!" said Norman. "I need a better idea."

Norman looked at the boxes of baked beans outside his mum's store.

"**That's it!**" he cried. "I'm going to beat the baked bean can stacking record. That will show silly old Derek!"

Mandy started the stopwatch. But she wasn't sure this was a good idea!

Meanwhile, Derek had found an old bathtub, and was pushing it up the hill with the help of Sarah and James.

"Do you really think you can get the world record for riding furthest in a bathtub?" asked Sarah.

"Of course I can," boasted Derek. "Now give me a **big push!**"

Derek sped down the hill and through the streets. "Whooooah!" he cried. Right in front of him was Norman with his tower of baked beans!

Smash! The tower crashed over, and cans flew everywhere!

"**Help!**" cried Norman, dangling from the bridge.

Dilys rushed outside. "Oh my poor boy!" she cried. "I'm going to call Fireman Sam."

Nee nah! Nee nah! Fireman Sam raced over in Jupiter.

Sam used Jupiter's tower ladder to rescue Norman from the bridge.

"Thank you for rescuing me, Fireman Sam," Norman said.

Then Norman sighed. "I was **so close** to breaking the record!" he wailed. "Now I'll never be a record breaker!"

"Hmm," said Sam. "By my count, that's the fifty-seventh time I've had to rescue you, Norman. Surely **that's** a record!"

"He's right!" said Mandy. "I guess you **did** break a world record after all!"

THE END

Book of Records

Now it's your turn to set some new records!
Ask an adult to help you fill in the records.

1

How many hats can you balance on your head?

_____

How many times can you kick a football?

_____

2

3

Can you make a paper plane? How far can it fly?

_____

4

How long can you dance for?

_____

Did you set any records? **WELL DONE!** Colour in this medal.

Search and See

There's an emergency up on the mountain! Look carefully at this rescue scene to find all the objects.

Woolly and Lambikins

Flare

First aid kit

Wallaby One

37

Answers on page 67.

Story:
Sam and the Sandwich Rescue

You can help read this story.

Listen to the words and join in when you see a picture!

Charlie

Hannah

seagull

Fireman Sam

sandwich

Today  is taking out on his boat. has packed a for lunch. When he's not looking, a flies down and grabs the !

"Hey! That's our !" says .

rushes over to grab the ,

but the doesn't let go.

stumbles and falls off the side of the boat!

"Help!" cries .

 calls  right away.

rushes over in Neptune the Lifeboat.

 pulls  out of the water.

"Thank you, ," laughs .

"You rescued me ... and you rescued our

 !"

THE END

Sing-a-long with Elvis

Use your brightest crayons to colour in Elvis.
Then point to the things in his song!

I have a blue fire jacket,
And a bright yellow hat,
Sometimes I drive Jupiter,
And rescue Lion the cat!

Pet Puzzle

Which jigsaw piece is missing from this pet day picture?

Do you know any pets? What are their names?

Well done!

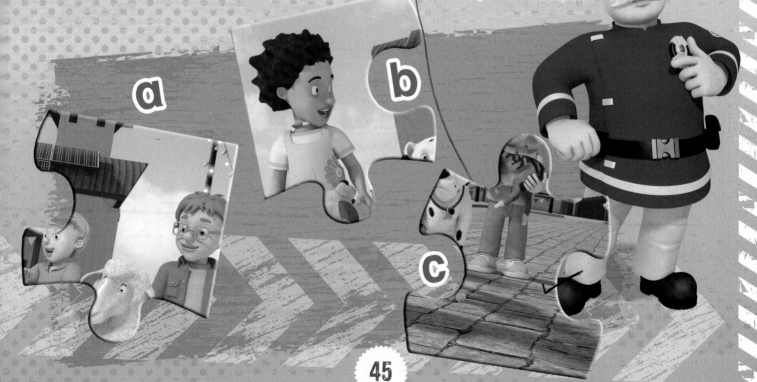

a

b

c

45

Story: Magic Norman

Read about Norman's magic show!

Norman likes to do magic tricks. He puts on a magic show for all his friends. "Ladies and gentlemen ... I am the Amazing Normanski!" he says.

Colour in Norman's magic wand. Then say "Abracadabra!"

Norman waves his magic wand.

"**Bappity-Boppity, Bippity-Bat**, I shall now pull a lion out of my hat!"

But Lion the cat doesn't like this trick. He leaps out of the hat, and knocks over the candles on the table!

The tablecloth catches on fire, but Nurse Flood knows what to do. "Everyone out!" she cries. "I'll call Fireman Sam!"

Trace the number Nurse Flood calls:

9 9 9

Brave Fireman Sam and Elvis put on their breathing apparatus and rush inside. They put the flames out quickly, and everyone cheers!

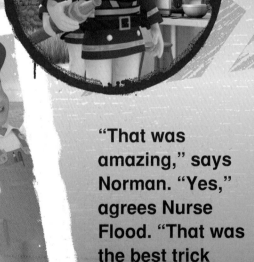

"That was amazing," says Norman. "Yes," agrees Nurse Flood. "That was the best trick of all!"

THE END

Let's Make Magic!

Norman likes to do magic tricks.
You can do a magic trick, too!

Materials:
- Scissors
- Crayons
- Tape
- Pen or pencil

This magic trick is an optical illusion. Your eyes fool you into seeing both pictures at once, so that Fireman Sam appears to be riding Juno!

Instructions:

1 Ask an adult to help you copy this page, and cut the rectangle out along the dotted lines.

2 Colour in the picture.

3 Fold the picture around a pen, and tape together.

4 Roll the pen very quickly between your hands. It will look like Fireman Sam is on Juno!

Race to the Rescue!

Can you help choose the right vehicle for each emergency? Tick the correct answer.

1 Nurse Flood's garden is on fire! Which vehicle should Sam drive to the rescue?

 Sailboat

Jupiter ✓

 Wallaby One

2 Naughty Norman is stranded out at sea! Which vehicle should Penny take to the rescue?

Mercury ✗

Ambulance ✗

 Neptune ✓

3 Sarah and Lily are trapped on a ledge! Which vehicle should Tom Thomas take on this mountain rescue?

Rescue Jeep ✓

 Juno ✗

 Bus ✗

49

Answers on page 68.

Hide-and-Seek

James is playing hide-and-seek! You can play, too.
Close your eyes and count: 1 2 3 4 5 6 7 8 9 10
Say, "Ready or not, here I come!"
Can you find James' friends?

Sarah ✓

Mandy ✓

Norman ✓

Lily ✓

Answers on page 68.

Odd One Out

Elvis is cleaning up the fire equipment. Can you help him find the odd one out?

Which one doesn't belong?

1
a    b    c    d

2
a    b    c    d

3
a    b    c    d

4
a    b    c    d

Answers on page 68.

The Great Pontypandy Bake-Off

Join the dots to see what the Sparkes family are baking.

Now colour it in and decorate it!

All About Juno

Juno is the Pontypandy Fire Crew's new jet ski. Juno has its own launch station so the rescue team can jump right into the water and hurry to anyone in need.

When Joe's go-kart crashes into the harbour, Sam and Juno race over to the rescue.

Colour in Sam speeding through the water on Juno!

Juno can go up to 50 knots through the water. That's very, very fast!

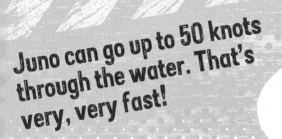

Er, what's a knot?

Can you think of something speedy like Juno?

A knot is a nautical mile. It measures the speed of boats!

Write over the letters!
Juno's speed is measured in:

knots

Story:
The Pontypandy Regatta

Now read about Juno's rescue!

It was the day of the **Pontypandy Regatta,** the biggest sailing race of the year!

"Everyone to their stations," said Fireman Sam. "I'll get **Juno** and start the race."

Down at the Quay, everyone was getting ready.

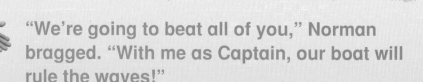

"We're going to beat all of you," Norman bragged. "With me as Captain, our boat will rule the waves!"

"No, *I'm* the Captain of our boat!" said Derek.

Norman and Derek were so busy arguing, they didn't notice the race was about to start!

"Ready... Steady... Go!" called Sam.

"Wait for us!" cried Norman. But the other boats were already far ahead.

"Now you're going to be the Captain in last place," Derek grumbled.

Up at the front, the wind had died down.

"Good thing I have my brand-new invention," said Joe. "It's called The Windmaster 2000. It will blow us right to the front!"

"Are you sure this is a good idea, Dad?" Hannah frowned.

But Joe didn't listen. He turned on his machine at full power.

Whoosh! The Windmaster 2000 was very strong. It knocked Joe right out of the boat!

Splash!

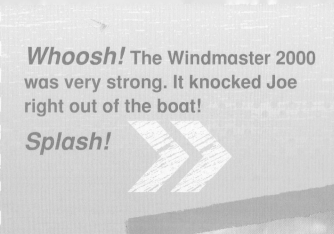

Fireman Sam raced over in **Juno**. He helped Joe back into his boat.

"Thank you, Sam!" said Joe.

"Now we're really far behind," Hannah sighed. "We should change the name of your invention to the Embarrassing Dad Machine."

Now Mike Flood and Elvis were in the lead. But Mandy and Sarah were catching up!

"Quick, Mike," said Elvis. "We need to steer to the port side."

Mike was confused. He tried to turn the boat one way. Elvis tried to turn the boat the other.

"**Look out!**" shouted Elvis, as the boat began to wobble.

"Aaah!" cried Mike, as he tumbled over the side.

"Arrrgh!" cried Elvis, as he tumbled over the other side.

Sam powered up Juno again. It was turning into a *very* busy day for Juno!

Fireman Sam made his way to the **finish line**. There, Mandy and Sarah were neck-and-neck with Trevor and Dilys.

"Don't let them past, Mandy," Sarah said.

"**Aye, aye!**" Mandy called. She steered the boat and knocked into Trevor's boat.

"Don't you bump my Trevor!" Dilys said. She bumped Mandy back. "Take that!"

As Mandy and Dilys bumped each other's boats, they steered **further** and **further** away from the finish line!

"OK, Norman," Derek said. "You can be the Captain."

"You're only saying that because we're about to lose," Norman said, sulking.

Norman and Derek didn't even notice that they were the only ones left! They **sailed** through the finish line.

"And the winners are ... **Norman and Derek!**" Sam announced.

"We won?" said Norman. "I mean, **we won!** Captain Norman is the winner."

"No, Captain Derek!" said Derek. "Fireman Sam, who do *you* think is Captain?"

Sam just laughed. "I think ... it's going to be a very long day!"

THE END

Pontypandy Regatta Game

Who will be the first to sail to the finish line?

Play with a friend. Roll a dice and move from space to space.

START

If you land on ...

Juno: Go forwards 2 spaces

Buoy: Go backwards 1 space

Neptune: Have another go!

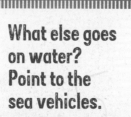

What else goes on water? Point to the sea vehicles.

Tip: Use buttons or coins as pieces.

FINISH

63

Penny's Patterns

Help Penny complete the patterns below by drawing in the picture at the end of each line.

What comes next?

Answers on page 68.

Mercury's Winter Rescue

Take Mercury the Quad Bike to rescue Mandy by racing along the track with your finger. Count the snowmen along the way!

START

FINISH

65

There are

snowmen

Answers on page 68.

Counting with Tom

Help Tom Thomas count the rescue equipment, and write the number of each item in the boxes below.

Saturn	Rescue Jeep	rope	walkie talkie	torch
5	3	5	6	4

Answers

Pages 12-13

Titan is red.

Page 21

I - c, 2 - a, 3 - b

Page 24

Joe's hot-air balloon is a circle.

Page 25

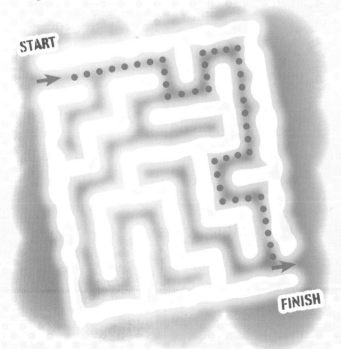

Pages 26-27

Pages 28-29

Venus is red like Jupiter.
Jupiter has 2 sirens.

Page 37

Answers

Page 45

Puzzle piece C is missing.

Page 49

I – Jupiter, 2 – Neptune,
3 – Rescue Jeep

Page 50-51

Page 52

I - c, 2 - b, 3 - d, 4 - c

Page 64

1   3

2   4

Page 65

There are 8 snowmen.

Page 66

Saturn – 5
Rescue Jeep – 3
rope – 5
walkie talkie – 6
torch – 4

FIREMAN SAM

LOOK OUT FOR THE NEXT EXCITING ISSUE OF FIREMAN SAM MAGAZINE!

3 GREAT GIFTS

SPECIAL ISSUE

FIREMAN SAM

Helps develop EARLY YEARS SKILLS

PLUS GIANT POSTER + PLAYMAT

40 STICKERS!

EXCITING WHALE WATCH STORY TO SHARE

Issue 103

6 PIECE PLAY SET

SPECIAL HEROES ISSUE

FIREMAN SAM

Helps develop EARLY YEARS SKILLS

2 SUPER STORIES TO SHARE

✓ WRITING
✓ COLOURING
✓ COUNTING

BE A HERO!

Sam will save the day!

40 STICKERS INSIDE!

PLUS HERO MASKS TO MAKE

Issue 107

EGMONT

INSIDE

2 GREAT STORIES

ACTION POSTERS

LOTS OF STICKERS!

COLOUR WITH PENNY
Colour over the holes to fix the leaking hose.

Are you ready?

COLOUR THE CREW
The firefighters are running safety checks on their equipment. Colour the picture and you can help too!

Safety first!

Can I help, Fireman Sam?

FIREMAN SAM TO THE RESCUE

FREE GIFT WITH EVERY ISSUE!